# Kitty's Special Job

Claude Clément
Adapted by Patricia Jensen
Illustrations by Olivier Raquois

Reader's Digest Kids
Pleasantville, N.Y.–Montreal

Every morning, just as the sun came up, the rooster crowed mightily and woke up all the animals on the farm.

"Cock-a-doodle-doo!" he shouted as loud as he could. "Cock-a-doodle-doo!"

"Woof! Woof!" answered the dog, running into the yard.

"Cluck! Cluck!" said the hen, as her chicks pecked at their breakfasts.

Proudly, the rooster looked around as all the animals started their busy day. All but Kitty, who was still asleep on her little pillow.

The big rooster scurried over to the sleeping kitten.

"Kitty!" he crowed furiously. "Didn't you hear my wake-up call?"

"Yes," Kitty said with a yawn. "But why do you wake us so early in the day? I'd much rather sleep."

The rooster stamped his foot. "It's my job to wake everyone on the farm!" he said. "What you need is a job, too!"

Kitty thought about what the rooster had said. "Maybe I could help wake everyone up. Then I would have a special job, too."

So Kitty took a deep breath and tried to crow as mightily as the rooster. But the only sound she made was a tiny mew.

The other animals laughed merrily at Kitty.

"Forget it, Kitty," chuckled the dog. "Cats just don't have special jobs."

"What's your job?" Kitty asked, feeling hurt.

"I watch the house and farm, day and night," the dog replied. "If any thieves try to come near, I bark and scare them away."

"I can do that!" Kitty thought. "Then I would have a special job, too."

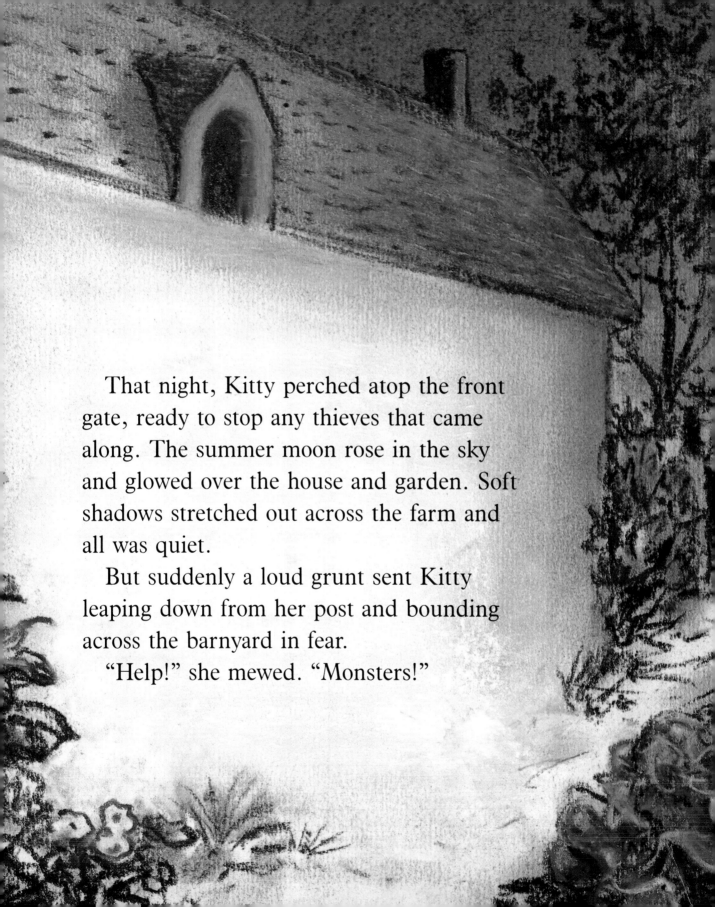

That night, Kitty perched atop the front gate, ready to stop any thieves that came along. The summer moon rose in the sky and glowed over the house and garden. Soft shadows stretched out across the farm and all was quiet.

But suddenly a loud grunt sent Kitty leaping down from her post and bounding across the barnyard in fear.

"Help!" she mewed. "Monsters!"

"Quiet down!" clucked the hen grumpily. "What are you making so much noise about?"

"There are monsters in the garden," Kitty said breathlessly.

"Nonsense!" snapped the hen. "That was only the pig returning to his pen. Now please be quiet so I can lay some eggs before morning!"

Kitty watched the hen flutter back to her nest. "Maybe I can lay some eggs," Kitty thought brightly. "Then I would have a special job, too."

So Kitty crept into the chicken coop and waited patiently to lay some eggs. But when she woke up, there was nothing beneath her but crushed straw.

Kitty sadly walked into the barn. There was Grandfather Cat, carefully watching a mouse hole.

"What's wrong, Kitty?" he asked, looking up. "Why do you look so sad?"

"I want to have a special job like the rest of the animals," Kitty cried.

"Why, Kitty," Grandfather Cat said, "you do have a special job."

Just then, they heard a noise in the corner. Some tiny mice crept out of the hole, hoping to steal the farmer's grain.

In a flash, Kitty pounced, frightening the mice away.

"Good, Kitty!" Grandfather Cat exclaimed. "Now you see, cats have special jobs after all! Without you and me, those mice would steal all the farmer's grain."

Kitty purred proudly. "I like my special job, Grandfather," she said. And, feeling happy at last, she curled up on a soft blanket and fell sound asleep.

Cats have excellent eyesight and can see very well at night. However, cats are thought to be color-blind.

The cat's large ears can tilt and twist to hear noises too quiet for human ears to hear. Cats may jump at a loud noise because their hearing is so sensitive.

Cats sniff everything around them to see if other animals or people have been by. Then they rub against things to leave their own scent.

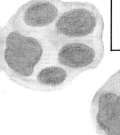